Not Your Average Princess Bellarose

Not Your Average Princess Series

B. Sunflower

Copyright © 2026 by B. Sunflower

All rights reserved.

No part of this publication may be reproduced, distributed, or transmitted in any form or by any means, including photocopying, recording, or other electronic or mechanical methods, without the prior written permission of the publisher, except as permitted by U.S. copyright law. For permission requests, contact Author B. Sunflower at authorbsunflower@gmail.com.

The story, all names, characters, and incidents portrayed in this production are fictitious. No identification with actual persons (living or deceased), places, buildings, and products is intended or should be inferred.

Book Cover by B. Sunflower

First edition 2026

Contents

Content Warning

Authors Note

Blurb

Dedication

1. Prologue
2. Bellarose
3. Melvin
4. Adonis
5. Bellarose
6. Adonis
7. Bellarose
8. Adonis
9. Bellarose
10. Melvin
11. Adonis
12. Gideon
13. Bellarose
14. Adonis
15. Bellarose
16. Bellarose

Epilogue

Afterword
About the author
Also by B. Sunflower

Content Warning

This book contains themes that may be sensitive for some readers and is intended for persons eighteen years of age or older. If you feel the following subjects may be distressing, please prioritize your peace and skip this book. Your mental health is important to me so proceed with care.

Sexual Assault / Rape attempt (on scene)

Mental Health Struggles (PTSD, Depression, etc.)

Burn Victim

Amputee Victim

Murder

Loss of Parent

Alcoholism

Sexual Content

BDSM (light)

If you feel I have missed anything charge it to my mind and not my heart. Feel free to reach out to me at authorbsunflower@gmail.com and let me know what may have been missed so I can update the warnings.

If you or anyone you know are suffering from any type of substance abuse or mental health issues please reach out to SAMHSA (Substance Abuse and Mental Health Services Administration) available 24/7, 365 days a year.

https://www.samhsa.gov/find-help/helplines/national-helpline

1-800-662-HELP (4357)

Authors Note

Okay, now that we have all the serious things out the way let's get into it. This is book two in the Not Your Average Princess Series. The entire series will be able to be read in any order. All the books will be novella's so please do not be mad at me because you wanted more information. You can however, reach out to me on my socials and ask me questions about any characters you are curious about and I will gladly engage with you. The hardest part about writing a novella is keeping it a novella. I understand the frustration of wanting or needing to know more, trust me.

Now it's time to get into this book. I'll talk to y'all a bit more at the end. Happy reading!

Blurb

Bellarose is perfectly content with her life as the beloved, curvaceous librarian of Covington. She's wise, empathetic, and unafraid to challenge convention, especially when it comes to rejecting her ex and the town's charming yet narcissistic butcher, Gideon Wilshire. Her quiet, book-filled world shatters when her father, Melvin, fails to deliver a commissioned painting to the secluded and feared Prince Adonis Habsburg. Known as "The Beast," Adonis is a man consumed by anger and trauma, his handsome face marred by deep scars from a brutal war. When he throws Melvin into the castle dungeon, Bellarose, in a moment of selfless courage, offers the Prince a desperate bargain. She will become his wife in exchange for her father's freedom. Now isolated, Bellarose must navigate Adonis's temper and the pain behind his scarred exterior. She's drawn to the mysterious man hidden beneath the mask, challenging his self-rejection and fear of vulnerability in the most unexpected ways. As their connection grows, Gideon, fueled by jealousy and entitlement,

begins to spread rumors to turn the villagers against the prince.
Will love be enough for them to stand against an entire kingdom?

This book is dedicated to my mom. I love you beyond measure. The relationship that we have been able to build means more to me than you know. I wouldn't trade you for the world. I love you forever mothaaaa!

Prologue

Prince Adonis Habsburg

Five Years Ago

"My Prince, you're the only hope that we have left for the kingdom. You can't leave to go fight this battle."

"So, you think I'm a bitch. You're telling me that I should tuck my tail and run. Turn a blind eye to a kingdom that has not only kidnapped my mother and is doing only gods knows what to her but killed my father and sent me his head!"

"I should cut out your tongue for even speaking such nonsense to me. That is my mother, and until her head is sent to me as well, I will believe she is still alive and remains the reigning queen of this kingdom! I am leaving this castle, and I will save my mother and if any of you try to stop me It will be your heads sent to your families to grieve!"

My father's incompetent aid irritates me to the max. I honestly don't understand why he keeps him around because his advice has always been subpar. Either way it doesn't matter, like it or not I don't give a damn, I am going to rescue my mother and burn down the kingdom in the west.

Our kingdom (Covington) is in the North. Our country is made up of four kingdoms split evenly, north, south, east, and west. There was to be peace amongst us, and we were to work together to keep the kingdoms strong.

According to the treaty signed, no king should bear arms against the other. If so, war would ensue. Though the king of the west did not outright bear arms against my father, he kidnapped his wife. In my opinion that was enough to start a war. My father died trying to save his wife. He didn't manage to save her in the end, but he did take out at least half of the other kingdom's soldiers.

Before my father left all the staff that were involved in assisting the other kingdom with their plans were sent to the dungeon. That was until I received my father's head on a platter. My betrothed, Elizabeth, was there and instantly fainted.

Anger like no other coursed through me. I could feel the rage seeping through my pores. I couldn't feel the hurt and pain at the time. I didn't have time to process it. I had to act. I had to release it. Everyone involved will die.

That same day while holding my father's head on a gold platter I looked at my seven Knight Commanders. "Take as many troops as possible to set up a perimeter around the castle in the west. I want it to only be one way in and one way out. Leave a wide enough opening for me. If it's not me and my mother coming out, they die on site. Set that shit ablaze and I'll come out through the fire.

"But sir what about the innocent ones in the castle?"

"Guilty by association. Fuck em'."

After that I walked to the dungeon leaving the ladies maids to tend to Elizabeth. With my father's head still in hand, I stepped into the light of the dungeon.

"Listen up, I need everyone in here to step to the front. There has been a change of events."

I waited until all these slimy motherfucka's came to the front of their cells. There were around eight women and twelve men. Uncovering the tray, audible gasps began to be heard. *Interesting.*

"Oh, don't look shocked now. This is what y'all wanted right. My father's head in exchange for your fucking greed. Even with your stupid ass betrayal he was going to see you imprisoned for the rest of your days. Now he can't see shit because he's dead. Now all of you must die."

As soon as my last words were spoken the guards came and began to unlock the cells. There was one cell that many did not know about and that was exactly where all of them were about to go. Tears and screams of forgiveness rang out. I didn't give a damn because this is the effect of what their greed caused.

You see this cell only had two walls and bars with a cell door. The opening at the back was a cliff with long jagged edges protruding out and if by chance you survived that there are some not so friendly mountain lions and bears that are pretty hungry around this time.

Once they were all packed in like sardines in the one cell I pulled my sword. *Swish.* My blade went across through the first person's neck like butter and their head hit the ground with a sickening thud. Music to sooth my troubled heart.

The others began backing away out of fear. Perfect. They completely forgot about the cliff behind them. They can try and run but their only option is death. *Swish.* Another head, and then another. Then screams being belted out with gasps of air in between. *Ah, the first of many to fall. Well, deserved.* This went on until there were none.

After cleaning my sword, I looked at my guard. "Let's head out." With that I was on my way to save my mother and end the kingdom of the west by any means necessary.

***

Upon arrival we breached the castle and made our way inside. The road here was filled with sights that would bring any man to their knee. The stench of blood and death was heavy in the air. Once we were inside of the castle all the knights that were not assigned positions outside were split up to search the castle. I made my way to the king's quarters and found the king of the west standing proudly with a smirk on his face and his sword drawn.

He began to speak as if anything he had to say was going to change his fate. “Ah, the prince has arri…” *Swish.* I didn’t want to hear anything he had to say. He said enough when he sent me my father’s head. Now to find my mother and then this place can burn.

I knew the king’s chamber wouldn’t be far from the queens, so I just had to find the exact room. After flinging a couple doors open, I found a nursery with my mother on the floor holding a baby. One of her legs was missing and she looked battered and bruised. My heart sank but the anger within me was stronger than any sorrow that could enter my soul.

My mother is the most caring, loving and attentive person in all the land. For someone to harm her for greed, power, and status is diabolical. I wish I could bring that sorry excuse of a king back and give him the slow death he deserved.

As I approached my mother, she slowly opened her eyes. She seemed to be pretty weak. Suddenly her eyes got wide and simultaneously I heard her gasp look out at the same time I saw a figure coming swiftly towards me from my right side.

I had just enough time to cover a portion of my face, but it was too late. A raw scream broke free from me and blazing heat dug into the skin along the right side of my face. I wildly swung my sword, my adrenaline at an all-time high. I can hear my mother screaming for me. I could only see through one eye. My skin was ablaze and then my mother yelled for me to get to the bathing chamber to rinse my face.

I suppose no one was leaving this war unscathed, even me. The kingdom of the west has fallen, father the king of Covington has been slain. The queen, my poor mother, had her leg brutally chopped off and I have been doused with acid. Everybody gotta die.

I made my way half blind to my mother and she still had the child clutched in her arms soothing him.

"Help me up son. As you can see, I cannot walk on my own for now."

"Mother leave the child we must go."

"I will not. We will keep this child, and I will raise him with the love that he deserves as a prince. That winch cared nothing for her own baby. You might as well accept him as your little brother because that is what he will be. I know what they did to your father."

A lone tear slid down her face. As stoic as she appeared, you could see the pain beneath the surface.

"They killed him in front of me. He made sure to remind me in his last breaths that he loved me and would rather it be him than me any day. He died with grace and dignity. I never saw this for our future but here we are. This will not break us. I won't allow it."

Little did she know, I broke the moment my father's head was presented to me on a platter. How could I ever be the same loving and kind person I used to be.

***

One month later

"Adonis, we need to talk."

"About?"

"About us and the future of this relationship."

"Elizabeth, I don't understand what there is to discuss. We are set to be married in two months."

"That's the issue, Adonis. You cannot expect me to truly marry you now."

"Actually, I do. I don't understand the issue. We are in love and have been set to marry for over a year."

"I am a beautiful, well sought after princess. You were a handsome prince at one point but that has changed. Every time I think of the idea of kissing you or even looking into your face while having sex, I feel disgusted. At one point your value was higher than mine, now it is not. I prefer to marry up, not down. My ride should be here now to take me back to my kingdom. I have already sent word to my father, and he agrees with my decision. No one wants to be with a man that has the face of a beast. Though I will say that one side is still handsome. You might be able to fool the right person if you cover yourself, but not me, Adonis. I love you but I can't do this. Goodbye."

There was nothing for me to say. What could I say? Should I have begged her to love me past my scars? No, because she is right. My mother was excited for this union because then I could be crowned king and she could step down as queen and raise my little brother freely. Unfortunately, that will never happen. I am no longer the man I used to be. The anger inside of me is constantly at a simmer right below the surface waiting to be released on its next victim.

PTSD, anxiety, and depression. The skin across the right side of my forehead, right cheek, and around my right eye is heavily scarred. I have significant hyperpigmentation in some areas and hypopigmentation in others throughout my right side. The scar tissue left tight contractions on my face making it appear pinched.

My right eye has a dense, white opacification over the cornea (cornea scaring) causing vision loss in it. The surrounding skin is damaged by scarring. My nose has significant structural loss mostly on the right side of the bridge and the tip, while the right side remains more intact.

That was my straw that broke the camel's back. Through all the pain and heart ache I thought I had her. I thought I was still worthy of her love. I'm done. If I ever marry it will be of convenience. Not love. She can never know the real me nor will she ever see my true face. Love doesn't live here anymore.

Bellarose

"Bella, I'm going to have to head out to see the castle soon and meet with Prince Adonis. I didn't finish the painting that he has already paid me for, I just need more time."

"Dad, what do you mean you didn't finish the painting? You and everyone in this kingdom knows how the prince is. Why would you agree to the job and not follow through?"

“I know, I know Bella. I honestly thought that I could do it. I just got so lost in thoughts of your mother while I was working on the painting. My life hasn’t been the same since we lost your mother. She was my heartbeat. Now it seems the only things that bring me comfort are you and the bottle. It seems this time the bottle got the best of me.”

“I understand dad, losing mom was hard on us both. You have to quit all this drinking though. I know you meant no harm and had good intentions, but you have to work through this. I miss the father that I had before the drunken nights at the bar and you stumbling in after one of your benders.”

“You used to be the fallen king's favorite artist and now you're the village drunk. You can do better than this dad because you are better than this. I’m still here. I still believe in you. I still and always will love you. Am I disappointed in you, yes, but that doesn’t change my love for you. Just give the prince his money back and I’m sure that will smooth everything over.”

“That’s the thing, I can’t.”

“What do you mean you can't?”

“I spent it all on alcohol and gambling. I know he’s going to have my head.”

“I don’t even know what to say. You need to figure this out, and fast. I need to get ready to head to the library because I’m opening today. I love you dad, please be safe and let me know when you get there and when you are headed back.

As I exited our apartment I pushed the thoughts of my father to the back of my head. He means well but he has been lost ever since my mom Monica died in the war five years ago. That was the same year that the king was killed. Now the kingdom of Covington is ruled by Queen Angela until her son Prince Adonis marries. We haven’t seen much of the royal family ever since the war ended. When we do see them, silence falls and respect is given.

Much has changed with the royal family since the war. The Queen now walks with a cane. Of course, it only enhances her beauty because she found a way to make walking with a cane appear elegant and graceful. Now the prince is a different story. The war seemed to have turned him into a different beast altogether.

If the rumors about his treatment of others and his quick to anger temperament are true, then he is a different type of beast to have to deal with. The war changed him. Before the war he was known to be a patient, kindhearted, and understanding man. Now he is known for being short tempered, ruthless, and cold-hearted. My father chose alcohol to ease his pain, and I guess the prince chose anger.

As I walked up to the doors of Covington's main library, peace settled over me. This is my happy place. Well, any library could be considered my happy place. Books are everything to me. Sad, mad, happy, doesn't matter, I will find peace in any situation within a book. I guess it makes sense that I would be a librarian.

Dressed in my favorite 1950s style tea-length blue dress with my gold heels, I unlocked the doors to the library and stepped inside. After cutting the lights on and preparing for the day I headed over to the checkout desk. Today is Wednesday and I'm expecting a rush of school children to come today.

My coworkers hate Wednesdays. I, on the other hand, love them. This is the time when their minds can be perfectly enriched. Seeing the wonder in their eyes while they are taking in all the information before them is nothing short of amazing. Right on queue at 9am sharp the kids begin to roll in. Time to get this beautiful day started.

My day was smoothly coming to an end. All the kids had a great time today and were able to sit in on a book read by one of their favorite children's authors.

Once I was done cleaning up, I closed and locked everything up and headed over to the butcher shop. I never look forward to going there because my ex is the owner. Unfortunately, he owns the only butcher shop in town. The day that he gets some competition I will fully support that person's business. Until then I have to continue to deal with Gideon Wilshire and his sexist and entitled ways. The crazy part about it is he is loved by the people of the town. They see him as this charming handsome man that gives back to the people. Being honest, he is all those things. However, he is a narcissist.

He has a way of making you feel small, not enough, and beneath him. He needs to be seen and on a pedestal at all times. I was captured by his charm initially. Thirty days into the relationship I was over it. He wants a servant not a partner. He seeks to control everything and when he doesn't get his way he throws a temper tantrum. I stood outside of the butcher shop and braced myself for the interaction that I was about to encounter. As I walked in the door chimed, making Gideon look up from the customer he was currently helping. He flashed a smile my way and I felt nothing but disgust. For the sake of keeping things cordial, I gave a small smile back at him. Once the customer left his full attention was on me.

In his smooth baritone voice, he greeted me. “Bellarose, how are you, my love?”

“Gideon, I told you to stop calling me that. I am well though. I just need four ribeye steaks, one rack of lamb, and one pork shoulder.”

“Straight to business I see. You know things don’t have to be like this between us. I was the best thing that ever happened to you.”

“Gideon, can you please just fix my order for me please. I don’t want to get into this with you. We are too different and it will never work between us.”

“You see that’s where you are wrong. You just need me to teach you your place. Your father is a weak man. That’s why your mother was in the military instead of him. I’m here to help. Anything you need you know I got you Bella. You were scared the last time and I got it. You won’t have to work anymore, and we can have a ton of kids and live off the land.”

"So, you think I would fall into your arms after you insulted my father. Just give me my items so I can go please."

"Here, I'll give you the items because business is business at the end of the day but let me make this clear Bellarose. I gave you the time you needed to get your head on straight. Times up, you will always be mine whether you want to believe it or not. You and I are forever until the day we die. We can hash this out the easy way or the hard way. Either way the result will be the same. You will be mine."

Snatching my items up, I walked out of his store and stormed home. I really need to learn how to hunt and butcher food for myself because I refuse to continue to put up with him. Even though it's just me and my dad, I began to order more meat at a time to make my interactions with Gideon few and far in between.

"Hey, thanks for coming by. I really wanted to relax and watch this movie with you. My dad is out at his new favorite place, the bar, and I didn't feel like being alone tonight."

"It's all good. I don't smell any food though."

I looked up at him and scrunched my face up. "That's because I didn't cook. I do have snacks though. If you are hungry, we can order some food."

"Naw if I get hungry you can cook."

Gideon and I have been together a month now and I was really beginning to get tired of his shit. I think the only reason I have kept him around as long as I have is because the sex was slightly above average.

"Not happening, I had a long day at work today and I don't feel like cooking."

"I told you to quit your little job. How do you think it makes me look with you working in that stupid library?"

"I don't care how it makes you look because you don't work there, I do. And from what I can see, I love it."

"See that right there is why we have problems. Your mouth is always moving faster than your brain."

My jaw was on the floor. "Get out, Gideon."

Out of nowhere he was on me with his hands around my throat screaming at me.

"You had me come all the way over here just to not feed me or give your man some pussy. You crazy as hell if you think I'm leaving without one or the other. You

choose which one I'm getting or ima choose for you. But I must say my preference would be that sweet little pussy that I've come to love."

I was frozen in place and gasping for air. How did I not see this side of him? He chased me for years and made me think he was this charming gentleman only to find out that he is a monster.

As scared as I was at this moment, I refused to submit to him. I will never fold against a piece of shit like him. I know my worth and he is clearly not on my level.

He took his other hand and caressed my breast and smoothed his hand down my side. As if I was about to stand here and get into him trying to force himself onto me.

"No, you can get out and get out now."

He laughed in my face and grabbed me harder around my neck.

"If you think you bout to keep what's mine from me you got me fucked up."

Realizing he wasn't going to let up I threw caution to the wind and said fuck it. I kneed him right in the balls and then quickly grabbed my gun that I kept under my end table.

Pointing it at him I calmly stated, "I asked you nicely to leave, now look at you. Bent over like the Hunchback of Notre Dame. Gideon, would you please be so kind and get your shit and leave before I have to shoot your ass. I don't want to, but I will. Also, if kneeing you in the balls and holding you at gun point isn't enough indication, we're done."

Every time I see that man's face I think about the last day that we shared together. Outside of my mother's death, that was one of the worst days of my life.

Melvin

Covington's castle sat at the top of the highest peak in the entire kingdom. It was about a two-hour drive from where I live. Along the drive, thoughts of the situation I found myself in plagued me. Which in turn made me start thinking of my love.

Monica Rozita Carmichael, the love of my life. We had been together since grade school. I was always a naturally awkward person but that never bothered

Monica. I was getting picked on one day in school and she came over and put the boy in a headlock until he cried uncle and promised not to mess with me anymore.

That was third grade. In eighth grade I asked her to be my girlfriend. When junior prom came along and I saw her walk down the stairs in her pretty pink prom dress. I knew she would be my wife and we were going to live happily ever after together like all the people do in the books that my Rose reads, but that didn't happen.

War took her away from me. It didn't surprise me one bit when Monica told me she wanted to join the military. It was right up her alley. A fighter with a caring heart of gold. She was a nurse and her unit specifically was sent out to war to help the injured.

I've always viewed my wife as an unstoppable force. But I guess something as small as a grenade can take out anyone. When I got the news something inside of me broke and for the life of me, I haven't been able to put the pieces back together. To lose your best friend, confidant, lover and wife all in a matter of seconds is a feeling that I wouldn't wish on my worst enemy.

That woman took my entire life force with her when she left the world. Now I just feel like I've been existing and not living. I have had numerous thoughts about taking my own life, but when I sit with my thoughts I know in my heart that Monica wouldn't want that for me and neither would our precious daughter.

It may not seem like it to most people but every day that I get up I try. Hell, just getting up is commendable because if I'm being honest, I could smile everyday but subconsciously I'm waiting for the day that I go to sleep and don't wake back up. I wake up and feel a weight on me like never before. Memories of joyful times bring me sorrow. One day I woke up and picked up a bottle, and I haven't put it down since.

I want to stop but I don't know how and I can't do it on my own. Hearing Rose say she was disappointed in me hurt. I needed to hear it though. I have to change. Even if it's not for myself. She has already lost one parent, and I know it would crush her to lose me so soon after losing her mother.

I don't know what's going to happen when I speak with the prince but whatever it is I just hope he has mercy on me.

Adonis

Jab to the face, cross, hook to the ribs. Uppercut, cross, 1-2, slip, 2, duck and move, duck and move. 1-6-3-2, pivot, 1-2-5-2.

I was in my room shadow boxing. This has become my morning routine to help me try to clear my head. I am proficient in many styles of fighting, though the sword is my favorite. It has a sense of historical skill that many don't appreciate.

Most people use guns nowadays. While I can shoot a cotton ball off a rat's ass and the rat will live to tell the story, I find no pleasure in it. There is no physical showmanship of power and strength behind a gun. ***(Knock, knock, knock.)***

"What is it?"

"Um, your highness, Mr. Carmichael is here about the painting you commissioned him to complete of your father."

"Fine, I'll meet him in the parlor in a minute."

After the staff member left, I finished cleaning myself up and headed to the parlor with hopes that the painting of my father turned out nicely. I wanted this to be a gift for my mother. Even though she appears to have handled my father's death with grace I know she has been suffering and missing him deeply.

As I entered the parlor, Mr. Carmichael immediately bowed and I permitted him to rise.

"Well, let's not waste time. Let me see it."

"Ugh, well my Prince, here's the thing…I didn't finish the painting."

I stared at this imbecile as if nothing he said registered. In all honesty it didn't because there is no way he is standing here telling me he hasn't completed a painting that I paid in full up front and had three months to complete.

"So, you've come to return my money then. Hand it over and leave while you still can Carmichael."

He makes an audible gulp that lets me know his next words just might be his last.

"I came to ask for more time. You see I have hit a bit of a creative block. This project brought back so many memories of my late wife. I just became consumed with grief. You see, I lost my wife during the war. She was one of the head nurses. Now it's just me and my daughter Bellarose. She's been holding everything together for us since my wife's passing. Ever since I got the news, I haven't been able to paint the way that I used to.

"So, you want me to feel sorry for you is what I hear."

"No, not at all my, Prince."

My anger is boiling for so many reasons at this point.

"You knew before I commissioned you to do the painting that you were unable to paint. Yet you took my money and as a man looked me in my face and said that you would get the job done. Do you think I can't smell the alcohol seeping out of your pores! I'm going to go ahead and assume you don't have my money."

Smirking as I think of his punishment, it comes to me. "Maybe you need a good detox. You, take Mr. Carmichael here to the warmest part of the dungeon that we have. We're about to start a little detox program."

"After an hour put him in the cliff hanger and he will be on a diet of pork, trout, black beans, sunflower seeds, pumpkin seeds, chia seeds, and spinach. If he's on good behavior he can have a little dark chocolate for a little razzle dazzle. He is to only have unsweetened coconut water as a beverage eight times per day. Take him."

"No! Please, you can't do this! What about my daughter? She won't know what has become of me. Please! At least let me call her and let her know that I am now a prisoner. Just one phone call please."

His crying only irritated me more. "Fine. He may have one phone call but after that your days will be spent in the dungeon alone thinking about your life choices."

The only thing keeping me from killing him was the fact that my father was a fan of his work. That was the reason I commissioned him in the first place. If he thought, I was supposed to have sympathy for him he was sadly mistaken. The whole of us as a kingdom suffered during the war. Yet we all had to push through no matter how difficult. He needed to either drop his nuts or suck them up and figure it the fuck out.

Bellarose

I received a call from my father last night stating that the prince is holding him prisoner. Instead of going to work, I had to call out to head to the castle to request a meeting with the prince to see if there was anything that I could do to get my father released. I don't know how this will go but I have to try. He is all I have left in this world, and I refuse to lose him.

Once I arrived at the castle the guards were not trying to let me inside to see my father.

"Sir, I am trying to be as respectful as I can but if you do not let me inside to check on my father you will be taking me inside to be held prisoner right beside him for assault."

"Ha, on who? I suggest you leave while you have a cha…"

Wap Wap

I popped him clean in the mouth and then hit him with an uppercut while standing gracefully in my cute gold stiletto pumps. I'm not typically a violent person but I was not leaving. I was going to see my father by any means necessary.

"You split my goddamn lip winch."

"Winch? Oh, I should've hit you harder."

"That's it. Let's go." Another guard came over to cuff me and began to haul me inside.

They brought me in through a separate entrance that led straight to the dungeon. The stairwell leading down was dark and ominous. It seemed as if it was a never-ending journey until I heard soft sniffles. I paused for a moment only to be snatched forward by the guard. They placed me in the cell and then turned to me.

"You wanted to speak to the prince so badly, well now you'll get your wish. I think you just might regret it." Chuckling he walked away leaving me there.

Still hearing the sniffling, I called out. "Dad? Dad? Is that you?"

"Rose?"

"Yes, it's me dad. Are you okay?"

"Ah well, I'm as good as a man who is detoxing could be, I guess. Where are you? I can't see you. Wait, is this in my head?"

Chuckling I said, "No dad. I'm not in your head. I got sent here because I punched one of the guards in the face because they weren't allowing me to see you."

"Bellarose, you did what! Why would you do that? The prince is going to have your hide. Lawd, Rose I swear, you know how the prince is, why would you do something like that?"

"Yup, I know how the prince is just like you knew how he was before you failed to complete the painting for him. You knew when you called me that I would come here and at least make sure you were okay. You are all I have left and I cannot lose you."

“I know Rose, I know. I don’t know when or how I will get out of here, but when I do, I will be a changed man.”

The sounds of vomiting began to echo throughout the dungeon. “Dad, what’s going on?”

“Oh, just detoxing very hard over here.”

Boom!

The door to the dungeon flew open and hit the wall and there stood the prince. I’ve only ever seen old pictures of him, and they were before the war. I don’t know why he has this Phantom of the Opera vibe going on, which is one of my favorite books by the way, but he is very handsome. Is he handsome enough for me to bite my tongue, absolutely not.

“Finally, why would you have my father call me to let me know that he has been arrested but then not allow me to come and check on him. He is sick and struggling in here. He has vomited twice since I have been down here. His body cannot handle this. You need to let him go, please.”

“Hmm, let’s unpack everything you just laid on me as if you are the one in charge here. I allowed your father to call you because he asked. That was a grace I extended because of the friendship he held with my father, which is also why he isn't dead. I could have let you go throughout the rest of your day not knowing a damn thing. I don't have to allow you to do shit up in here because this is my shit not yours. Do I come to your home making outrageous demands of you, no. Your father committed a crime. He essentially stole from me. Unless you have the bread, he owes me then he will remain here. His body can't handle much of anything because his ass is alcoholic. I was kind enough to put him on a diet that would help with him detoxing but do I get any credit for that, nope. Instead, you stomp your little ass up to my home and have a temper tantrum because you didn't get your way. Now look at you, in jail. I should bend your pretty ass over my knee."

"You will not touch my daughter!"

"Oh,

your nuts trying to drop now? Good shit. I'm proud of you. Don't get shit twisted though. I will ball your old ass up and not think twice about it. Send Ms. Red here home, she light work."

I can't let him keep my father here. He needs real medical help. "No, please, I'm sorry. Please let my father go."

“Now why the fuck would I do that Ms. Red?”

“I can take his place. Punish me instead. I can handle it, I promise. Please, just punish me, not him.

“Rose, no. Don’t listen to her. I’m old, she has her life to live.”

I got down on my knees, tears in my eyes, bearing my soul to this man. I could not lose another parent.

“Please my prince, keep me instead, punish me not him.”

Silence descended over the dungeon for a while as everyone anticipated his response. I crossed every finger and toe I had with the hopes that he would keep me instead. I watched and waited as he pondered over everything that I said. I also watched as his tongue came out and went across his perfectly white teeth.

“Fine.”

Simultaneously my father yelled “No,” as I yelled “Yes.” Then the record scratched when the prince continued with an evil smirk on his face.

“On three conditions.”

Adonis

The excitement in Bellarose's eyes went away as soon as I said there would be conditions. If she thought this would be an easy trade, she had me messed up. Her father played in my face and her coming here thinking she was going to make demands and get me to bend to her will just because she shed a few tears was laughable.

I will say though, her being on her knees begging me to punish her had me ready to brick up but I fought it off as best I could. Ms. Red was breathtaking. It doesn't matter though.

As quickly as those thoughts came to mind, I dismissed them.

"Conditions?"

"Yes, conditions Ms. Red."

"Why does it sound like this will only be beneficial to you?"

"Well, that depends on perspective."

"Rose, don't do this, please."

Her father's whining was really starting to irritate me.

"Hey, Melvin."

"Yeah."

"I'm going to need you to shut up before I cut your tongue out." He audibly gulped and shut up real quick.

"Back to the conditions. First, you must marry me. Second, an heir must be made between the both of us. Third, his drunk ass gotta go to rehab if I release him. The only reason I am even still extending him grace is because I can't have my future father in-law out here making us look bad."

I heard nothing but crickets in all directions. Did they think I was playing?

“Are you serious right now?”

“As a gunshot wound to the chest.”

“Why should I even consider marrying you?”

“You don’t have to. I really don’t give a damn either way but if you don’t his ass stays here and the offer will be off the table.” I shrugged because I really didn’t care either way.

The offer that I gave was one that would be convenient for me. I needed to be married, and she dropped into my lap. There is no need to try and woo her or sway her one way or the other. These are the facts. She either took my offer or didn't. Was Ms. Red beautiful? Hell yeah, she's gorgeous. Freckles intricately placed over her light creamy brown skin. Full lips with a mouth that I wouldn’t mind having wrapped around my dick. Don’t even get me started on her fiery red hair. If you thought black people couldn’t have natural red hair, she was living proof in the flesh. Did any of this make me feel like I needed her or would bend for her? Fuck no. This will be a marriage of convenience and nothing more.

“Fine, I’ll marry you.”

“Cool, take him to the nearest rehabilitation center.” The guards unlocked his cell and began their struggle to remove him from the dungeon.

“Wait, no. No, please. Don’t do this. Leave me here! Don’t take my daughter please!” Melvin continued his ranting until it slowly began to fade away. I turned back to see Ms. Rose shedding a few tears.

Unlocking her cell, I looked down at her. “Let’s go, Ms. Red”

Bellarose

It's official, the prince is an asshole. He didn't even give me a chance to give my father a hug or anything before he sent him away. I can only hope that it won't be the last time I see his face.

I followed behind the prince with my head hung low as I wiped a few of my tears away. That was until I heard the rapid patter of feet approaching. I stopped in my tracks and turned to look and see a cute little boy running up to me.

“Hi, you’re pretty.”

“Well, aren’t you just the cutest. What’s your name?”

“My name is Prince Charles Habsburg.” He said that with the biggest grin possible.

“Oh, my apologies young sir.” I did a dramatic bow for good measure causing him to break out in laughter.

“Wanna be my princess?”

Before I could respond Adonis was at my side replying to his brother. “Sorry little brother, but you’re a bit to late. She’s to be my bride.”

His handsome little face looked offended. He leaned over and whispered into my ear, “You would choose him over me? I’m nicer and I know where the cooks hide all the good snacks.”

Chuckling I pulled him in for a hug and told him, “Unfortunately, I’m stuck with this one over here.” I made sure to cut my eyes at the prince when I said that part because he needed to know that I wasn’t going to make this easy for him.

“I guess, but if he gives you any problems let me know and I can beat him up for you.”

“You wish you could beat me up.”

“If I can’t mama will.” After sticking his little tongue out he ran off to only god knows where.

“Seems like you can be a decent human. Does that only apply to your little brother?”

I could tell my question annoyed the prince, good. “For your rude ass information, I have always been a decent human being. My mama ain’t raise no slouch. For you to think such things of the queen is wild.”

“Oh, it’s no disrespect to the queen at all. That’s reserved for you.” Did I just see a smirk on his face? No way.

“That pretty little mouth of yours is going to get you into trouble Ms. Red.”

“I hope you don’t think I’m scared of you, because I’m not. Don’t think because you’re a prince that I’m going to just bend over and kiss your ass.”

“Oh no worries. I’ll be the one doing the bending.” He winked at me and I was equally disgusted, humored, and turned on. The turned-on part threw me off though because I refuse to like this man. I might have to marry him, but I don’t have to like it. Right?

We finally stopped at a door and Adonis motioned for me to open it. Opening the door, I was surprised at how grand it was. The room was completely decked out. The color scheme was navy blue with golden yellow accents throughout the room. The room looked fit for royalty.

Stepping inside I took it all in. A large California king bed sat to the left of the room. Straight ahead was a beautiful love set and coffee table set which set in front of a bay window. To the right I noticed two doorways. Both doorways were wide and arched; however, one had double doors that opened outward and the other had no doors at all. I decided to see what was behind the closed doors first.

After opening the doors and audible gasp left my mouth. It was a closet. Well not just any closet because my father and I both could fit our entire lives inside of here and every possession that we own would only take up a corner of space. My mind was blown.

"I will have the seamstress come today to take your measurements to get clothing made for you. You can have the entire right side of the closet." I had completely forgotten about the prince for a moment until he scratched my record.

"The right side as in we are sharing a closet?"

“I knew you were smart.” The urge to knock him upside his head set heavy in my spirit but I knew he had a thing for beheading folk, so I tried my best to keep my hands to myself.

“You look so much better when you’re not talking.” I noticed him flinch a bit, but he quickly recovered.

“You look better when you’re not acting like an entitled ass, but here we are.”

“Excuse me! How dare you? You’re one to fuckin’ talk mister I’m going to hate the world and every living creature that exists because my daddy died. News flash Prince, you’re not the only person that lost someone dear to them due to the war and it doesn’t give you the right to treat people like shit because of it!”

Should I have spoken to him that way, no, but he had pushed me and I was over biting my tongue. Within a blink of an eye he was standing over me with his hands around wrapped around my throat. He squeezed my throat and then eased off a bit. Leaning in he began to speak.

“You’re right Ms. Red. Unfortunately, though, I was the only one who had their father’s head personally delivered to them and had to find his mother abused and chopped up like she was nothing. You damn right

I'm angry, but the next time you speak to me like that you will be punished and it won't end until I see tears of regret running down that pretty little face of yours."

Adonis

"Mm, mm." I heard a throat clearing behind us. Turning around I saw my mother standing in the doorway. She raised an eyebrow at us and we instantly pulled apart.

"This must be the fiancé that your brother spoke of. I was unaware that you were engaged son. Introduce me."

Rose's face began to turn red. I grabbed her hand and she instantly snatched it away. I chuckled a little because she is going to pay for that later.

"Mother this is Bellarose Carmichael, daughter of artist, Melvin Carmichael. The marriage was just arranged not long ago, and you were going to be the first to find out of course. I would like for us to be married as soon as possible so we can begin working on an heir."

My mother's silence was excruciating. She just stood there blankly and then turned her eyes to Bella.

"And what would you like my dear?"

"I would like to knock him upside his head, but I believe those types of actions are unbecoming of a future princess, so I'll settle for tripping him every chance I get." My jaw hit the floor. I can't believe she said that to my mother.

My mother seemed to be amused at her response. "Oh, I like her. She's the perfect woman for you."

"Oh, so you think the perfect woman for me is one that will give me hell every chance they get?"

"That's where you're mistaken, son. I think the perfect woman for you will not be afraid to call you on your bullshit but also hold you accountable for your actions or lack thereof. It seems you have met your match and I'm glad. Bellarose, it has been a pleasure, and I look forward to telling you all the embarrassing details I can remember of Adonis."

"Mother!"

"Oh, hush now. You better relearn how to be nice because I don't think you will have a choice in the matter." With that my mother walked out and I stood there confused.

I turned around to give Ms. Red a piece of my mind but she was no longer standing where I last saw her. Searching through the room, I found her back in the closet. She was looking through my clothes.

"What do you think you're doing?"

"I'm going to take a shower and since I don't have any clothes of my own here, I will be using yours."

"You can't just do that."

"Watch me." She snatched up a t-shirt and some basketball shorts and walked off to the bathroom. Then I heard the shower running.

Curiosity got the best of me. I had to see her. As much as I said this will be a marriage of convenience, I still had eyes. Something about little Ms. Red intrigued me so much. I couldn't quite put my finger on it though.

I walked into the bathroom to find her standing directly under the waterfall. I never knew my mouth could go dry so fast. The only thing that could quinch my thirst would be the water that was running down her beautifully sculped body. Her erect nipples had a reddish-brown hue to them, and I craved to just run my tongue across them at least one good time.

"You know they say staring is rude. I'm pretty sure your momma ain't raise you like that." Just that fast I was snapped out of it and annoyed with her smart mouth. Not enough to not want to join her in the shower though.

I didn't even bother to respond. I just undressed and got in the shower with her. I went to reach for her, and she smacked my hand away.

"Absolutely not." *What the hell.*

"What's up with that? You not scared for me to see you naked but I can't touch you. Were about to be married."

"And. You want a cookie? I'm marrying you to save my father but if you think you about to just slide up in me you got another thing coming. You will earn this good shit. Now be a good boy and pass me the soap please."

Oh, she got me fucked up. Without another word I stepped out of the shower and walked out slamming the bedroom door. I didn't give a damn that I was naked because not only was I hard as fuck for a woman who decided to make my life a living hell and we're only on day one, but her ass was not only making me feel shit, but she was also making me think.

This woman had my mind focused on her already and something was telling me that it was only going to get worse.

Bellarose

Adonis was about to be in for a rude awaking messing with me. People have an instant impression of me because of my style of dress. They assume that I have a demure, reserved personality. I do in certain settings, but I have never been a push over nor one to bite my tongue.

I will marry him but before he even gets to sniff me, he will respect me. And if he wants an heir as bad as I think he does he will fall in line either the easy way or the hard way. Part of me has a feeling he will choose the hard way.

Before he even knows it he will be on his knees for me. I'm already under his skin and I love it. He wants to hate me so bad but he can't.

As much as I hate to admit it finding out about how he discovered his father's death made me realize the prince has layers that I want to peel back. Maybe I can even help him heal those hurts.

An idea begins to form in my mind. I just have to figure out how to execute my plan to get to know the prince.

Later that evening a slew of clothes were brought to the castle for me including lingerie that I intended to use to seduce the prince.

While in my room in the closet helping the staff arrange the clothing in the closet a knock came at the door. I hadn't seen Adonis since he got mad at me earlier and I'm pretty sure he wouldn't be knocking at his own door. I walked over and opened the door to see another staff member with his slightly bowed.

"Good evening, madam. The royal family requests your presence for dinner."

"Thank you so much. Can you let them know I will have to pass this time. I'm not quite hungry but if they are having breakfast together in the morning I will definitely be there."

"Oh, okay. Will do madam. Thank you for your time." The gentleman tipped his head slightly and left as fast as he came.

The other staff left about five minutes later and I took another shower, dressing in a sexy gold lingerie set and got in bed. I had no idea which side of the bed Adonis preferred, and I didn't care at the time because I was exhausted. Today had been a long day with a lot for me to process.

Adonis was right in the fact that things could have been way worse for my father due to his actions. By law he could have killed my father due to theft from the royal family but he didn't. Instead he locked him up and forcing him to detox. Putting it all into perspective I realized I owe Adonis a thank you. He's helping me. It may not be my ideal way of helping but it works. Because of him my father is getting the help that I couldn't afford to provide for him. For that I am grateful.

I was rudely awakened to bright lights being cut on in the room and Adonis hollering my name.

“Rose, get up! Why would you not come to dinner?”

Ugh, does he have an off switch? “Adonis, it would be great if you left me the fuck alone.” I rolled over and turned my back to his nonsense.

I should have known that him leaving me the hell alone wouldn’t happen. This man walked over and snatch my covers right up off me. I turned to look over at him, and he was standing there with lust in his eyes.

His eyes slowly caressed my skin. He started at my ankles and made his way up my legs and thighs. He took a dramatic pause once his eyes reached my ass. I can admit that I didn’t have the biggest ass out here, but she sat pretty and round.

For no other reason besides taunting him, I decided to make one of my ass cheeks jump. He moaned and bit his lip.

“You know starring at people is considered rude.”

“Am I not allowed to stare at what’s mine?”

I turned over before answering, giving him full view of my breasts covered in sheer lace. The growth that I saw in his pants let me know that I needed to tread carefully. It was so hard to act unbothered after seeing his body in the shower. He had the smoothest light brown skin I've ever seen. I'm not ashamed to admit that the sight of his dick alone had me ready to let him twist me up like a paper clip. The odd thing about it all was the fact that I still have not seen him without some sort of mask covering half of his face.

"I wasn't aware that I belonged to you yet. We haven't exchanged any vows yet."

"Ah, you are sadly mistaken my red rose. The moment you agreed to this arrangement you became mine." He inched closer to me, and I know I was turning red with each approach. Even with that knowledge I refuse to lose this battle of wills against him.

I allowed him to get close enough where I could feel the warmth of his breath graze my skin. I looked up into his eyes and noticed a difference in the one behind the mask. It was a cloudy sort of white color. I reached up and placed my hand gently against his mask.

Just as fast as the moment came it was gone. I must have triggered something within him because Adonis began to pace with his chest heaving up and down.

"What's wrong? Did I do something wrong? Did I hurt you?"

"Why would you touch my face in that manner? What do you know?"

"I have no idea what you are talking about. I touched you because I am intrigued by you and for some crazy ass reason you turn me on."

He laughed, "Right, that's believable. Are you sure you're not here to see the monster behind the mask."

"What the hell are you talking about. Be so for real. I am here because I traded places with my father. You made this proposition not me. If anything about you is monstrous, I would have to say it would be your nasty ass attitude. I told myself that I was going to try to make the best of this situation. I was even lying in here thinking about how, even though the way you went about helping my father wasn't ideal, you helped me. I was going to thank you for all you've done so far. I was going to try to be more understanding of you and try to meet you halfway in this marriage but fuck that. If you are content with being an asshole toward the person who is not only set to be your wife but the mother of your damn kids, then I'm done."

With that I threw on a robe and left out the room. I didn't know where I was headed off to in this huge castle, but I knew I needed some space from this man. He was driving me crazy,

Melvin

I hadn't seen or heard from my daughter in two weeks. I can only hope that she is doing well. All that I can do at this point is wait until I can reconnect with her once I am released. When my brain is clear I think back on what transpired at the castle. I am grateful to the prince but in those moments I was not.

I even went as far as bashing him and let her ex-Gideon know that the prince had taken her from me before I was taken to the facility. He said he would handle it, but I am not sure what that entails but I do regret my words. He hadn't taken anything from me. My daughter volunteered in place of me. If it were not for my actions, she would never have been in this situation. Now that my first two weeks are over, I'll be able to call people.

The first thing I'm going to do is check on my Rose. If all is well then I will let Gideon know that she is safe and there is no need to worry.

Adonis

It's been three weeks and nothing has moved forward in the direction of a wedding. Bellarose refuses to cooperate with anything about planning or getting fitted for a wedding gown.

Worse than that my mother and little brother are entertaining it and taking her side.

I've never had the urge to apologize to a person before, but this woman is getting to me. I understand that I may have overreacted to her touching my face, but I couldn't handle her rejection. I've heard rumors about the monstrous prince. They started not too long after my ex left me. Then the rumors grew and my monstrous actions became what people thought were the monstrous parts of me.

No one except close staff knows of my injuries and far less have ever seen my face to even be able to say what I look like. The one person that I was comfortable around without my mask made me feel like I was no longer worthy of love because of my disfigurement. That it was the first thing that people saw and was now going to be the thing that people remembered me by. Not the me that was at my core.

As much as I hated to admit it, Rose was right when she refused to have a child when she and I cannot communicate effectively. Selfishly, I refuse to let her go so I will try to be the bigger person and get to know her. She has avoided me like the plague, but I have had eyes on her and have learned that she is a librarian. Well, a former one because no wife of mine will work in a public library.

If she wanted to start up organizations or nonprofits in the realm of books, I would be all for it, but she will not be working for anyone. Soft girl life and all that shit the women be talking.

The staff informed me that she was currently in the gardens where she frequently reads books that she requested to be brought to her. I decided to go meet up with her and give her a little treat as an apology for my behavior.

I stepped out into the garden and took in the aroma in the air. The blend of the various natural fragrances of vanilla, honey, lemon and lavender, instantly began to put me at ease. I almost forgot that my mother created a sensory garden. It has been a long time since I have been here. The garden incorporated the traditional five senses, vision, hearing, smell, taste and touch. All types of plants were thriving back here.

Of course I would find my red rose lounging in the gazebo, smack dab in the center of the garden. Once she looked up and spotted me, she rolled her eyes so far to the back of her head you would have thought she was possessed.

She watched as I bent down to pluck a few honeysuckles. As I walked up to her, I maintained eye contact with her as I licked the droplet of the head of one of the blooms. I caught the slight shift in her thighs as she pressed them together.

It might be taking her mind a bit longer to get with the program, but it seems her body is already there. Maybe me apologizing will help her brain begin to catch up. Ms. Red looked beautiful. Her vibrant natural red hair shined in the light of the sun. Her freckles along with her outfits of choice gave an appearance of a woman who was innocent and soft spoken. Hell, even her job title gave off that impression. However, my red rose was none of those things and looking at her, I am beginning to realize that.

She demands my respect and submission just as much as I demand it from her. I am not used to submitting to anyone but for some odd reason she makes me want to try.

"For you, Ms. Red."

"Are you trying to poison me?"

"Seriously? You just watched me pick the damn thing. Stop being dramatic woman."

"I will stop when you stop being an ass."

"Look, Rose, I apologize okay. You were right about some of the things that you said. I grew up surrounded by the love my parents shared and after so much loss and hurt I decided to protect myself from ever letting anyone in. Let alone physical intimacy. I cannot honestly say that I am ready for you to touch me, but I am willing to try. You can touch me anywhere but not my face."

"Before you were an ass to me, I wanted to thank you. I guess since you're being a little sweet, I can let you know what I am thankful for. The day I came to the castle was the first day I spoke to my father without alcohol in his system since my mother's death during the war. Though it is sad that it took something this extreme to give him a wake up call I am grateful for how you handled the situation. I guess you could call it a necessary evil."

I smirked at her and slowly fed her a honeysuckle. She responded with a slight moan at the gentle sweet taste. "So, I hear you have a love for books."

"Well, you heard right."

"Come with me." Without giving her a chance to object I grabbed her hand for her to walk with me.

"Where are we going?" She asked with a lighthearted giggle.

"You'll see when we get there nosey." Of course that made her roll her eyes. But this time it wasn't anger or annoyance, so I'll take that.

We walked through several corridors to reach our destination. Before we made it to our designated door she stopped in front of the large red door that sat beside the one, I intended to take her to.

"What's this room?"

"This room is off limits. If I catch you snooping around there will be consequences."

"There you go again getting all dark and mysterious on me. Just come on and show me whatever it is that you trying to show me."

I could tell that not being transparent bothered her, but I wasn't sure if she was prepared for what was on the other side. I haven't explored the other side of that door since before the war. Though the idea of going in there with her does something to me, and by something, I mean makes my dick jump.

Finally making it to our destination, I wasted no time opening the doors for her. The look of awe on her face made all this worth it. Ms. Red took off and left me standing in my spot. She ran her hand over almost every book that she could reach. She was surprised to find a lot of indie black authors on the shelves. The royal library is where I took her. We have currently about twenty-eight thousand books on hand but can easily hold up to about sixty thousand. Each level of the library has stairwells to reach them as well as an elevator. There were five levels in total.

I let her explore as much as she wanted without interruption. I honestly think that she forgot about me. As I watched her, I sort of felt like the Grinch when his heart started to grow. The thought of her possibly being able to make me happy seemed farfetched but something was happening here.

I found her in a bay window style book nook located on the third floor of the library. I remember this being my favorite spot to come to with my mother when I was a kid. Looking at her tucked away nice and comfortable with a book in her hand and the sun shining down on her beautiful face and hair had me in awe.

"You just forgot about me huh?"

"Nope. How could I forget the man that is voluntarily miserably engaged to me. I just chose better entertainment."

"Okay, I guess I deserved that."

"You deserve that and more, but I digress."

I chuckled a bit because I am beginning to enjoy her feistiness. "Listen, I don't want to fight anymore. We need to figure this out. Plus, for some reason I think my mother might be on to something."

I grabbed her hand and pulled her up to me. "You might be the one to tame the beast in me."

"Oh, you want me to tame you huh?"

"Only if you think you can."

Gideon

When I found out that the prince got hold of my Bella I was pissed. I already despised his ass. He killed off half of my family and now he plans to take my wife! I'm not having it. I went around to the town's people and let them in on the news of how the prince forcibly took my fiancé from me. I also made sure to remind them how he killed my family off. I had everyone meet at the library that Bella worked at to discuss the actions of our heartless ass prince.

"People of Covington, I hate to gather you all here under these circumstances but enough is enough. The prince once again has shown us what type of monster he truly is. He has already killed off half of my family just for being in the wrong place at the right time when his father was killed. Our king was a great leader, but I am afraid that if we allow the prince to take the throne, we will soon fall as a kingdom. "

"To make matters worse he is forcing my fiancé to marry him instead of me. You all know how much I love Bellarose and know that she would never agree to something like this. We have to do something. We must come together and request a public audience and demand that the prince be deposed for his past and present actions. His behavior will not stand in the Kingdom of Covington!"

Cheers and sounds of excitement at my words filled me with pride. I should be a royal. The people believe in me and follow me. These are my people and I deserve to have Bella at my side through it all. She is mine and mine alone. If he laid one fucking finger on her, I'm killing him. It's as simple as that. Melvin called me about a week ago and let me know that he didn’t mean what he said to me about Bella. That she volunteered and wasn’t forced. Fuck that and his drunk ass. I don’t give a fuck if she got on her knees and prayed to God himself for the prince. Them prayers won’t be answered if I have anything to do with it.

Bellarose

Things have been going great with Adonis in the past month. I actually look forward to waking in his arms. The only thing I look forward to more is seeing his face.

We still haven't had sex yet, but I want to and I know he does as well. The build up has been slowly coming to a head. The small touches, the intense looks of desire. Don't even get me started on the way I feel when I'm wrapped up in his arms at night and I feel his dick pressed against my ass.

Currently I was in the bathroom getting ready for bed. He was already in the bedroom, but I had a little surprise for him, so I stayed behind. I stepped into the room wearing a royal blue lingerie piece. Adonis's eyes roamed over my entire body as he took me in bit by bit.

"Damn."

"Come here." He looked up at me confused.

"Don't make me have to repeat myself Adonis. Now, come here. I want you to get on your knees at the foot of the bed and stay there, and no you cannot touch me." I added that because he will not touch me unless I can touch him.

He moved and got on his knees as I asked. "Good boy."

I sat at the end of the bed and leaned back onto my elbows then propped my feet on the bed with my legs spread wide open.

"Fuck you have the prettiest pussy I have ever seen in my life." He licked his lips in anticipation of getting a taste. He could see everything because my bottom half was crotchless.

I began to roll my hips and rub my hands up my body. I reached my nipple and pulled my top to the side and began to roll my hard bud between my thumb and pointer finger. I was so turned on I felt my essence running down to my ass.

"Let me clean you up baby."

"Why should I? Have you been good?"

"I've been so good. I'll be even better. Please don't torture me like this Red. I haven't had a nut since the day I laid eyes on you."

"You can get one lick, but if you go further this will end immediately. Before you do though, we are going to incorporate the traffic light signal. Green is great, yellow is a bit uncomfortable, and red is you want me to stop. I am going to push your boundaries Adonis." When I said that his head went down.

"Look at me baby." I never stopped touching myself the entire time. I was now rubbing my clit, and he zoned in on it.

"My eyes, baby, my eyes." Once I had his full attention I returned to what I had to say.

"Are you ready for this Adonis, because if I give you all of me, I need to have all of you." I stuck a finger inside me and stroked myself in and out slowly.

"I want all your good and bad. I want your light and your dark. Scares and all I want you. Even if those scares are internal, give them to me Adonis so I can make it better. Are you ready to lick you pussy?"

"Yes Ms. Red."

"Mm, I like that. Come lick it baby."

"Mm, shit. Good boy. You like that?"

"You taste like honey and I want more. Can I have more Ms. Red?"

I began rubbing my clit faster. I was about to cum. "I'll give you more. Stick out that juicy ass tongue and open that mouth nice and wide for me. Yup just like that." I rubbed my clit a few more times and then squirted right down his throat. And like the good boy he was he swallowed it all.

"You still hungry baby?"

"Hell yeah."

"Then eat that shit." No sooner than the words left my mouth he devoured me entirely. I almost forgot that I was supposed to be in charge here.

His beautiful hair was up in a man bun right now. He usually wore his hair out and flowing around his face. I grabbed a hold of his bun and began to rub my pussy all over his face and his mask. I don't know what type of tricks he used to keep that damn mask in place, but it didn't budge and I was honestly tired of seeing it.

"Take it off."

"Huh?"

"Take the damn mask off Adonis!" He froze at my words. Everything stopped. His eyes began to water but no tears fell.

"Adonis, look at me." He lifted his gaze for a moment and then looked away from me again. I grabbed his chin and faced him to me.

"I don't give a damn about what is under that mask, Adonis. I care more about what is inside of you. Admittedly when we first met, I thought there was nothing there but over the last couple of months you have shown me that you do have a heart. That is all that matters to me."

With his eyes on me a tear fell. "I'm scared. Hell, I can't believe I even just confessed that. You're not the first woman I was engaged to. Before you there was Elizabeth. She left me after the war because she couldn't stand to look at me and the thought of her kissing me let alone having sex with me disgusted her."

"I have no problem sitting my kitten heals to the side to beat her ass. What type of shit is that to say to a person you a supposed to love?"

"She didn't love me. She was marrying me because of status. She would've been marrying up but My face was permanently damaged during the war when I went to rescue my mother."

I lightly touched the side of his face. "Come here." He got up and leaned forward over my body. I began to place light kisses over the side of his face that was mask free. I slowly made my way over the side that the mask was on and began the same treatment. He tensed at first, but he relaxed after the fourth kiss.

I whispered to him between each kiss. "It's time baby. What's your color?"

"Yellow, Ms. Red."

I slid my hand down his chest and grazed one of his nipples. "Do you want to stop?"

"You can do this baby. I'm here. I'm not leaving you. Plus, something tells me even if I tried you wouldn't let me anyway." That finally got a smile out of him.

Reaching his hand to the back of his head I heard something click. He must have had some type of device custom made to keep his masks in place and his hair hid it well. With his other hand held over his face preventing the mask from falling, he slowly began to lower the mask.

I could see the fear of my reaction throughout his entire body. I saw the scars yes, but I finally saw him. He had nothing to fear because this moment allowed me to truly see him.

"Wow, you're beautiful, Adonis." He was shocked.

"You're just saying that."

"Actually, I'm not. You look better without the mask. You were hiding behind that mask for too long. The mask and past hurts and untreated trauma made you bitter and monstrous. Not the injury."

Adonis

I never knew it could be like this. I never saw love or even a true partnership with anyone after Elizabeth left me. I admittedly folded in on myself and pushed everyone even further away as a means to protect myself.

I never could have predicted this fiery woman coming into my life and turning it around. She has effortlessly shown me that I am still me and I can be loved as I am. Although we haven't expressed those words I feel it.

This is nothing like what I had with Elizabeth. This is work. This is earned. This…she, is mine, and I plan to show her in every way possible. Taking my mask off made me feel the most vulnerable that I have ever felt in my entire life. Yet somehow, I felt it was right to do. Over the past two months she and I have really got to know each other really well. I began to develop feelings for her before I even realized it.

Bellarose found a way to chip away at the wall I put up when others couldn't. She challenged me instead of catering to my every demand. She knew the risks and didn't care not one bit that with a snap of my finger she could lose her life. She saw me, and now she is seeing me with fresh eyes and accepts me for me.

After taking my mask off for her she began to pepper the same kisses all over my face the same way she did when I had the mask on. I was scared and it felt a bit funny because no one outside of a doctor touched my scares.

"Is it crazy that I think your skin feels softer on this side than the other?" Before I could say anything, she took her tongue and licked the side of my face from the bottom to the top. Then she kissed my eye. My blind eye. Most people don't realize that I am legally blind in one eye and I worked hard to not allow it to affect my day to day.

"Mm hmm. This side tastes better too. You're being such a good boy letting me see all of you. You want to know what it does to me when you're a good boy?" God, I have never been a sub, always a dom and in control, but this shit got my shit leaking like a faucet.

"Yes, ma'am."

"Feel your pussy baby" No words were needed. I worked two fingers inside of her and without my dick even touching her yet, I knew this is where I would call home. She had led this thing long enough and it was time for me to take over.

I snatched my fingers out of her mid moan and smacked her on the ass. "Get up and grab your robe. I'm taking you somewhere. Now isn't the time to ask questions either just hurry up and do it." I cut her off before she could even begin her questioning.

After she threw her robe on, I took her to the door near the library that she had previously questioned me about. I was the only one with a key to this room and I maintained the cleaning of it as well. Only one other woman had been in this room and that was my ex. Before I opened the door, I made sure to remind her that we were still operating on the traffic light system, and she was cool with that. I kissed her on the lips and opened the door.

I didn't frequent this room often, but when I did, a time was had. I haven't played in here in five years. I've had sex but this type of play requires a different level of intimacy and trust. I had all types of shit in here. Some I'm sure she knows of and some may be new to my little red rose.

Straight ahead along the back wall as soon as you open the door it was a St. Andrews Cross with stealth cabinets built into it. There was a large bed to the left with integrated tie down points built in. Toys were neatly stored in a glass display case for her choosing pleasure. Rose stood there with a shocked yet pleased expression on her face. I turned to make sure the door was secured and by the time I turned back around Ms. Red was on her knees with her eyes down without me having to tell her a thing.

"Good girl. I knew you had it in you. You've been a bit of a bad girl, Ms. Red. I won't be to hard on you because your stubbornness helped me in the end. However, you still will be punished."

"I'm sorry, sir. I'll be good next time I promise."

"Oh, you're going to be good now. Come here." I stood at the karma sutra chaise and watched her crawl over to me.

After getting her situated on the chaise I walked over to the display case to choose what will be used today. I decided to keep it simple since this was our first time playing together. I made sure to continue to gage her temperature as I went along.

I grabbed a suede flogger and a rose toy and walked back over to my soon to be wife. I let her know that everything was new and properly cleaned. I'm a nasty nigga but I'm not a nasty nigga. Holding the flogger in hand, I gently rubbed it along her body and watched as she shivered.

Using the flogger, I eased her robe up over her ass and it was a sight to see. "I'm suppose to be dishing out punishments but if this pussy keep juicing like this ima have to show it something." I took the flogger and swatted her on the ass with it.

"Ssss, yes. Please, show me something babe." She moans so pretty.

"I'll show you something if you give me your soul before I fuck you."

This woman looked me right in my eyes, no fear in sight and said, "I'm not giving you shit. Take it." Oh, she wanna be a brat. Cool.

"When you crying for mercy, I'm letting you know now I'm not stopping."

"I'm not… Shit!" Whatever she was about to say was irrelevant to me at that point.

I put the rose on her clit and shut her ass right on up. With the other hand, I was flogging away. We weren't even five minutes in, and she came twice so far.

"Ten. That's your number. Come for me ten times tonight and then I'll give you this dick babe. You think you can do that for me?" I sat the flogger to the side and massaged her with the rose still on her clit while I waited for her answer.

"Y yes, sir."

"Mm, good girl." After the sixth time she came, I couldn't take it anymore and started eating it from the back. At ten I came up for air and slammed right into her wet ass pussy. Her clit was so fat and swollen from all the attention I could feel her nub rub against my balls as I pounded into her.

This shit was amazing. “Got damn Ms. Red. Shit! You been walking around here all this time with confessional pussy!”

“Oh, my fuckin’ God! Yes! Yes! Don’t stop!”

“Oh, I ain’t stopping. This my shit ain’t it.”

“It’s yours, baby. Only yours.” I pulled out and sat down on the chaise and pulled her on top of me.

“Slide my pussy down on my dick then.” When she slid down on me, I heard birds chirping, the sun was rising, shit, the air even smelled cleaner.

She rode me like she was trained in barrel racing all her life. I reached up and grabbed her throat and squeezed just enough to get her attention and her eyes rolled in the back of her head from pleasure.

“We not planning a wedding anymore. We getting married tonight.” I wasn’t asking, I was telling her.

“Fuuuck!” She creamed all over my dick and my stomach.

“Hell yeah. You ready to be my wife ain’t you!” Her body kept convulsing.

I couldn’t hold back anymore, and I came so fuckin’ hard I think I pulled a fuckin’ muscle.

“Ugh, ugh. Get your ass up Ms. Red. I was dead ass serious. Throw your robe on. I’m about to call the officiant and tell him to wake his fat ass up so he can marry us. Then ima call my mama so she can be a witness."

"Adonis! What the hell? I'm not even dressed."

"I don't give a fuck. You think ima let you walk around with pussy that makes me wanna confess my sins and apologize for all my transgressions all willy nilly like that and not lock you down. You either marrying me today or I will literally lock your ass away Rose." Do you know her crazy ass laughed hard as fuck in my face.

"What the hell are you laughing at woman? I'm dead serious." I stared at her like the crazy woman she was as she tried to catch her breath from laughing so hard.

"I know you are serious and that's why I'm laughing. How could I say no to you and deny you endless access to your righteous pussy." She walked over to me, squeezed my balls and kissed me on my cheek. The side with the burns. Her favorite side and walked out the door.

We had an intercom system throughout the castle. I decided to say fuck the phone I'm waking everybody up.

Pressing the button on for an all call I spoke into the speaker. "A, Witmore, wake ya fat ass up right now. I'm getting married tonight. If you not downstairs in twenty minutes that's ya ass. Ma, I hope you ready for some grandchildren cause it's about to go down. Man, if I would've listened to you from the beginning I could've been felt that heavenly gushy… Ahh got dammit Rose. Why the hell you beating on me."

Bellarose

This crazy ass man was about to announce to the entire castle including his momma and little brother how gushy my damn pussy was. What the hell kind of pussy did I put on him. It was cute though. Seeing this playful carefree side of him is what hooked me.

Now here I am thirty minutes later standing in the great hall in some slippers and a silk robe with my hair all over my head about to marry Adonis. Who by the way is shirtless and barefoot with pajama pants on that have crowns all over them. His mother had on decent pajamas with a scarf on her head and the officiant looked like he was just here to make sure he's not sent to the chopping block…literally.

"Let's get this thing started Whitmore. I'm trying to get back to the confessional." I turned beet fucking red.

"Adonis!"

"Now I know dag on well you not talking about a church so I wish you would shut the hell up. I told your father fucking me pregnant while hanging upside down was going to fuck up your damn brain. Now you just don't know what to say out of your mouth I swear." My jaw was on the floor. I never could have guessed the queen would speak like this, but it was hilarious.

"Ew ma, what the hell. That's just wrong. You ever thought that maybe I get not knowing what to say from you, because you clearly couldn't figure out that no one needed to hear that shit." Ms. Angela or Ma, that she requested I call her, smacked him upside the back of the head.

"Would you come on boy. I'm tired and you got us up in the middle of the night because you got a taste of some good nookie and fell in love. Now that y'all are going to be married I expect to see the both of you in the morning in the hall for the public audience request that was sent."

I instantly got a bit nervous because for some reason it took that comment to make me realize I'm about to be a real-life princess. I took a moment and closed my eyes and thought about my mom. *Look at me now Mom. You raised me to be strong, a fighter, a lover, and smart and it got me this far. Thank you for showing me love and how to love before you left this world. I love you forever.*

"Bella." I was startled out of my thoughts by Ms. Angela.

"Yes ma'am?"

"Oh, hush all that I told you about that. Anyways, I don't want you to be nervous about anything. I know you can handle this life and anything it throws at you. When I first met you, I saw a bit of myself in you. You are poised and graceful, stern and steadfast. And if the broken nose I heard about you giving one of the guards is any indication, a true fighter when necessary." My cheeks grew a bit red at that.

"You don't ask for respect, you demand it. You were already made of true royalty, that's why I knew from the first day you would be an amazing wife to my son. I had the power to end this entire mess that Adonis here put you in. I was going to do just that until I heard you and him going back and forth with each other."

"In that moment I realized my son needed you more than you needed him. I want to thank you Bella. You saved my son. Five years Bella. It has been five years since I was able to lay eyes on his handsome face." All three of us began to get emotional at that point and we began to shed a couple of tears.

"On his wedding day, thanks to the care and trust the two of you have built together, I'm not only seeing his face, but I have seen him smile and heard him laugh. I am seeing him again because of you. Not all shero's wear capes but some do wear robes." I smiled because I never envisioned being a hero to anyone especially a man but here, we are.

"Well, my Queen, after that speech I think we can just skip right along to the I do's unless the both of you have something you want to say."

"Actually, I would like to say something." Adonis spoke up.

"I can't believe you were able to get under my skin the way that you did. You drive me absolutely insane in the best ways. You demanded my affection, attention, and respect above all else. You pushed me to be better and forced me to sit in my thoughts." Adonis paused and looked down for a moment and then looked back up at me.

Gently grabbing my chin and holding my face in place so that I could look into his eyes; he took his thumb and grazed along my jaw line and then my lower lip. Without losing eye contact he finally spoke again.

"Bellarose, you made me love you. And I'm not talking about love that can easily be forgotten. I'm talking everlasting, territorial, burn the world down, and cater to your every need for as long as I have breath in my body kind of love. If you ever try to leave me, remind yourself that you can't because you will forever and always be my little red rose."

Most people would probably say that it was at this exact moment that I realized he was crazy. But, in this moment I realized I was crazy too because everything he just said was so romantically sexy to me. That shit had me getting wet all over again. Let me hurry up and say my piece so we can get out of here. I'm tired of turning red out of embarrassment because I can't stop having lewd thought about my man.

"Adonis, I believe you live to irritate my soul, but that's okay because I will only allow one person in my life to do that and that is you. I will warn you though, I am as sweet as I am mean. I am as sane as I am crazy."

"You have earned my love, but it comes with the understanding that just as much as you would burn the world down for me, I will blow the shit up with the sweetest smile on my face as I sit and watch all of humanity disappear for fucking with you. You are mine just as much as I am yours and I will always stand ten toes behind you good or bad." Adonis and his mom both smiled at the little speech I decided to give. The officiant just looked at all three of us like we had lost our damn minds.

"Well, Prince Adonis Habsburg of Covington, heir to the throne, do you take Bellarose Carmichael to be your lawfully wedded wife?"

"Hell yeah." He smirked at me and it melted my heart.

"Bellarose Carmichael, do you take Prince Adonis Habsburg of Covington to be your lawfully wedded husband?"

"I sure do. As long as he knows that he's going to be the one to let his little brother know that we got married without him." Adonis jaw hit the floor because he knows his brother is about to be on his ass. His mom just laughed before she spoke.

"Oh, it's perfectly alright because if y'all thought we still weren't going to have a traditional ceremony you're wrong. We may be a little rough around the edges but we're still royalty and a show will be put on. Continue Whitmore."

"Right, I now pronounce you husband and wife. You may kiss the bride." The kiss was everlasting transcendence. I didn't want to come up for air, but we were still with his mom, so I pulled away after a few.

Adonis turned to his mom and kissed her on the cheek. "I love you mom and thank you for everything but we gotta go."

With that he grabbed my hand and we ran back to our room and enjoyed ourselves until the sun was about to rise.

Bellarose

I woke up to Adonis's hair tickling my face as he peppered kisses all over my face. "Wake up princess. It's time to start your royal duties. The first one will be attending your first public audience request. The staff will be in soon to help you get dressed. We will be matching of course, and you will have your pick of tiaras to choose from to go with your gown.

"Okay, okay fine, I'm up. Let's get this thing started." One last kiss on my lips and we both were off to get ready.

Two hours later I was dressed in a gorgeous sun kissed golden yellow velvet dress. It was the "Sacramento" design by Cathrine Walker & Co. Apparently, they were this "it" company for royal attire. The dress was floor length with strong padded shoulders. It had a dramatic thigh high side slit that almost reached my hip. The beading is what brought everything together. I truly felt like royalty.

As for the tiara, I decided to go with the Josephine Soir De Fete Ruby Tiara. The simplicity of it made it so beautiful. The single ruby stuck out to me because it reminded me of Adonis's nickname for me.

Queen Angela, Adonis and I waited for us to be announced before we entered the room and took our seats.

"My Lords, Ladies, and Gentlemen, pray silence for His Royal Highness the Prince of Covington Adonis Habsburg and his wife Her Royal Highness the Princess of Covington Bellarose Habsburg" You could see the shock on everyone in attendance as we stepped out.

I kept my head tall and held on to my man's arm because this is where I wanted to be and where I belonged. It also didn't go over my head that this is the first time that the people have seen my husband without a mask since the war. My man walked just as proud and strong right beside me and we took our seats.

"Her Majesty Angela Habsburg the Queen of Covington." She walked in with so much grace it was as if she was gliding across the floor.

Once she was seated, I finally let my gaze brush across the room. Who did I spot among the many…Gideon got damn Wilshire. Everything in my body wanted to tense up but I managed to maintain my composure thank goodness. That didn't stop Adonis from noticing something was off. He lent over and whispered in my ear.

"Are you alright Ms. Red?"

"Yes, we can discuss it later. No worries." I made sure to smile and put him at ease. We stopped talking just in time because the Queen cut her eye at us and then gestured for everyone to be seated.

Gideon was the first person to step forward. I had no idea why he was here but if I knew Gideon the way that I did I knew he was up to some weaselly ass shit.

"Mr. Wilshire, I understand that you and those around you have an issue with my son. What pray tell might that issue be?" If it wasn't such an intense and serious moment, I would have laughed because the three of us had the same reaction. We all lifted one brow in question awaiting his response.

"Well, Your Majesty, may I speak freely?"

"Please do."

"Your son should not be allowed to rule as King. He has done more than enough harm to the people of Covington as it is." Murmurs began throughout the room but the three of us remained silent.

"He has slaughtered his own people because he can't control his own temper. He behaves no better than the beast we all can now see with our own eyes that he is." I notice Adonis slightly flinched at that remark. Yet we all remained silent and allowed dumbass to continue.

I knew of all that my man had done because he bared his soul to me. At the end of the day, he did what needed to be done to save not only his family but this kingdom.

"I can attest to this because he slaughtered half of my family who was in servitude to this family for decades. Not once did I ever come here in retaliation. I kept my head down and catered to the people of our town through my butcher shop. However, now he has gone too far. He has forcibly taken my woman from me, only for me to find out today that he even went so far as to marry her. I will not allow this to stand."

The room became so quiet that I swore I could hear my heart beating through my chest. I was heated. No one could say anything unless the queen gave us an opening to say so again, I remained quiet.

"Mr. Wilshire, you have said a great deal today and I see that you have a way with words. So much so the people of this town have blindly followed you into this little snake pit you've gotten yourself into." *Oh shit.*

"Aren't there some things to your story that you are leaving out?"

"I am not sure what you are speaking of Ma'am."

"Oh, come now, Mr. Wilshire. Don't get close lipped on us now. As a matter of fact, how about we all speak freely here today." I am absolutely eating this shit up. All I'm missing is some popcorn. I just wanna yell out tag me in coach so bad right now but I'm trying to be very cutesy, very demure.

"My son did kill the shit out of your family. It brought me joy when I found out to be honest. Do you think I didn't recognize your family name? I know who you are and who your family were. But let us enlighten the people as to why my son killed off half of your family as you put it."

"My son killed them because your family was working with the king who had me kidnapped, raped and beaten then to top it all off…" The queen paused and lifted her dress, and everyone gasped, even me. She was missing part of her leg, and no one knew.

"My leg was chopped off in front of my husband only for me to be awaked after passing out to watch them chop my husbands head off." Not one time did the queen raise her voice. She spoke with stern certainty and authority.

"Mr. Wilshire your feelings about your family being murdered are irrelevant to me. I suggest you let that go unless you miss them so much, you're ready to see them again."

"Naw ma, you said we speaking freely, right? So, with all disrespect fuck him and his family."

"Okay well I freely said fuck you, you ugly mutant ass looking bitch." After Gideon said that you could see people beginning too slowly back away from him.

Before Adonis could respond I jumped in because he had me and my man fucked up. "Aye, let me tell you something Gideon. You will watch what the fuck you say about my husband because he isn't the one you will have to worry about. I broke up with you. I made it very fucking clear that it was over when your tried to force yourself on me and I had to pull my gun on you. I turned you down after that every time you tried to get back into my good graces."

"All you did for the few months that we dated was try to make me feel small and belittle everything that I did. You didn't respect me as a person and especially as a woman. You walk around here making the people of the town fall in love with a fake ass version of you. But the real you is an egotistical narcissist who doesn't understand that no means no. I am exactly where the fuck I wanna be. Right next to my fine ass husband."

"I'm letting you and everyone else know you better talk to me nice about mine because I will personally beat ya ass over my man. Y'all done pissed me clean off. What has he done besides risk his life to save this fucking kingdom? Oh, he yelled at you. Boo Hoo. Hell, he yelled at me too when we first met. Did I deserve it. Maybe. But that's a story for a different day. All of you need to go home and think for your damn selves. Y'all are like the blind leading the damn blind." I suddenly felt an arm wrap around my waist and the hardness of Adonis dick press against my ass.

He leaned down and whispered in my ear, "That shit was sexy as fuck. I'm about to wrap this thing up and go fuck you Ms. Red."

Then a scream rang out into the air. Gideon was bent down on the ground hollering in pain. Adonis slick ass done tossed a damn knife in this mans foot making him unable to move from the spot he stood in because the knife was imbedded into the ground. Oh well.

"You thought shit was sweet?"

"Fuck you!"

"No thanks. But man to man I understand why you stuck on my lady." Adonis simple ass turned around with a big ass smile on his face and started badly singing and dancing to Justin Bieber's song *Yummy*.

"Yeah, you got that yummy-yum. That yummy-yum, that yummy-yum. Yeah, babe, yeah, babe, yeah babe. Any night, any day." This man was rolling his body and everything. I was beet fucking red and his mother was hiding her laugh behind her hand.

This man was really putting on a performance like he didn't have a man crying in pain on the floor. *I love him.*

"Babe, can we get back to it please." He stopped and walked over to kiss me before going back to his murderous business.

"Right, so you gotta die."

"W what? Why?"

"What the fuck you mean why. You not only tried to rape my wife, but you continued to stalk her and make advances when it was made very fucking clear to you that she ain't want your ass."

"But…but she wasn't your wife then."

"Ask me do I give a fuck. You think her not being my wife at the time excuses your behavior towards a woman. I think the fuck not." Adonis then looked up to address the crowd.

"Let it be known that I held this man's family in the dungeon without harm up until the day that my fathers head was delivered to me. Let it also be known that he and my wife were no longer in a relationship prior to me even meeting her. Let it also be known that he has come before the royal family with false accusations and has blatantly disrespected the crown in multiple ways that you all have witnessed here today." At that moment Gideon decided to spit at Adonis's feet.

Adonis reared back and almost knocked that mans head off his shoulders. A tooth flew out of Gideon's mouth.

"As I was saying, this disrespectful piece of shit is about to die. Any objections? No, okay." Without giving anyone a chance to respond Adonis snapped Gideons neck so fast that if you blinked to fast you would have missed it.

"Now y'all get the fuck out and enjoy the rest of y'all day." He walked over to his mother and kissed her on the cheek. Then he came over to me, grabbed my hand and we walked out like nothing happened.

Epilogue

Bellarose

One Year Later

I looked around the ballroom with a smile on my face. Since being married to Adonis, the castle has become much livelier. We have events again like they did before the war. I was currently on the dance floor with Prince Charles. He became even more obsessed with me after he found out that I was about to make him an uncle.

I was currently pregnant with Adonis and I's first child, a boy who we will be naming after his late father. The queen has been a god send because I was so nervous about this pregnancy and how I would handle it. She has supported me every step of the way. Both her and my father.

My father was released from his rehabilitation program three months after Gideon was killed. He has been sober ever since. He even got back into painting and finally completed the painting that Adonis commissioned him for. I was so proud of him. He has since moved into the castle with us, and it has been a joy.

"Sorry to interrupt Prince Charles, but your king would love to have a dance with his beautiful queen."

"You might be the king now, but I will still beat you up, and don't step on my sisters' toes." Charles stuck his tongue out at Adonis before walking away and we both shook our heads and laughed.

My husband was the most beautiful man in the room. The smile on his face made it that much better. No mask on, hair flowing down his back wild and free is how I always want to see him. People don't realize how much it took for him to get to this point, but I do.

"Thank you for not allowing me to miss out on this feeling."

"What feeling, babe."

"Joy." Then he kissed me.

The End

Afterword

Y'all made it! I hope you enjoyed the ride. Bellarose was certainly not your average princess and the Habsburg family were definitely not your average royals. The queen was admittedly my favorite character. Who was yours? Who did you dislike the most? Let me know in your reviews.

Wanna connect with me or become apart of my ARC team? Use the link below and it will take you to all of my pages.

https://linktr.ee/authorbsunflower

About the author

B. Sunflower is an urban romance author blending genres into captivating stories. A Baltimore native, army veteran, mom and wife who lives between the realms of reality and book universe. She reads just about any genre but her top three are Urban Romance, Romantasy (because romance and fantasy together is magical), and Historical Fiction. Her love language is food and doesn't understand why it is not listed as an option in the first place.

https://linktr.ee/authorbsunflower

Also by B. Sunflower

King Nation Jr.

All my life I've been content with playing the field. I knew what love looked like. I came from a healthy two parent household engulfed in love. I knew that when I saw my forever person I would know instantly, and I would dive all in headfirst. Well, I found her and her name is Queen Jayla Mahogany Nation. She's my wife and mother of my future children and she doesn't even know it yet.

Jayla Bryant

Love, trust, and loyalty is all I've ever wanted to be surrounded by. Growing up in foster care it wasn't always easy to get that. However, I've always wanted better for myself. I worked hard and eventually walked across that stage with a master's degree, belly and all with my husband and sister in the crowd. I thought that feeling would last forever. Thought I had it all. Until I found out I was wrong. Then a demon of a man came along to show me how love is really supposed to feel.

Jazzmen Johnson

Confined by the constraints of high society. Offered up like prized cattle to any man that has the right amount of money and prestige that my father deems fit.

A hostage.

That's how I felt in this world. A well-kept hostage by the hands of my own father. All I ever wanted was a chance to live my life on my own terms. I never saw a way out of my situation.

That was until I met Giana and her brother Alijah Booker.

All Piddy O'Connor ever wanted was her happily ever after. She thought she had it until the love she thought she had was proven to be a lie and right before Valentine's Day. With her determination not to let her break up, ruin her weekend away, she sets off to the beautiful cabin in the woods that was originally meant for her and her boyfriend. What she finds will set the course for the rest of her life.

Come along for this short ride into Piddy's life and see what she gets herself tangled in.

PS her mama named her Piddy because she went into labor while playing a game of Pitty Pat with her cousins. Why is it spelled Piddy instead of Pitty? Because be for real, no one says it like that.

All books are available on Amazon and Kindle.

Happy reading! Until Next Time.

B. Sunflower

www.ingramcontent.com/pod-product-compliance
Lightning Source LLC
LaVergne TN
LVHW010931110826
845149LV00013B/2551

* 9 7 9 8 9 9 4 0 1 1 8 3 6 *